D

AROUND THE WORLD IN EIGHTY DAYS

JULES VERNE

www.bakerstreetreaders.co.uk

Retold by Tony Evans
Illustrated by Stephen Lillie

Newbury, Berkshire, UK
www.bakerstreetpress.co.uk

Published by Baker Street Press Ltd. in 2018
First published by Real Reads Ltd. in 2013

ISBN 978-1-912464-03-6

A catalogue record for this book is available
from the British Library

Typeset in Baskerville and Scala
Printed in China by Imago Ltd.

CONTENTS

THE CHARACTERS

Phileas Fogg

Phileas Fogg is a wealthy gentleman who is calm, clever and usually gets his own way. He bets £20,000 that he can go round the world in eighty days – over a million pounds in today's money. Can he win his huge and risky wager?

Passepartout

Passepartout wants a quiet life. He has just become Phileas Fogg's personal servant. Has he made a big mistake?

Detective Fix

When Detective Fix decides Phileas Fogg is a bank robber, he is determined to arrest him. Will he succeed? And is Phileas guilty?

Princess Aouda

Princess Aouda is intelligent and beautiful. Can Phileas Fogg and his companions rescue her before she suffers a terrible fate?

The Indian Guide

He is young and brave, and an expert elephant driver. He guides the travellers through a dangerous and difficult part of their journey.

Sir Francis Cromarty

Brigadier General Sir Francis Cromarty meets the travellers when they are in India. Can he help them save the princess?

Captain Speedy

The captain refuses to take Phileas Fogg and the others back to England on his steamship. How can they make him change his mind?

AROUND THE WORLD IN EIGHTY DAYS

At five minutes past six on the evening of the second of October 1872, Mr Phileas Fogg was sitting in a comfortable leather armchair in the Reform Club. To those who knew him, this would have come as no surprise. He was a gentleman of exact and predictable habits, whose life revolved around his luxurious London club and his large house at number 7 Savile Row. This was the hour at which he always played cards with a group of five other wealthy men, and as usual they were discussing the news of the day before their game began.

Andrew Stuart, the famous engineer, held out a copy of *The Times* and pointed to an article on an inside page.

'It seems that this bank robber has got clean away,' he said. 'And with £55,000 in notes! He was a well-dressed gentleman, by all accounts, and simply walked off with the money after distracting the cashier.'

Gauthier Ralph, who was one of the directors of the Bank of England, shook his head. 'He will not get far. The money was taken on 29th September – that is only three days ago. All the ports are being watched by the police.'

'I don't agree,' Stuart said. 'After all, the world is a big place, and with that amount of money he can go anywhere.'

Phileas Fogg raised himself from his chair. 'Perhaps not as big as it was! You can now travel round the world ten times as quickly as you could a hundred years ago. According to today's *Morning Chronicle*, now that the new Indian railway has been completed it is possible to circle the globe in just eighty days.'

Mr Fogg picked up a copy of the *Chronicle* from a side table, and opened it so that his companions could see the chart on the third page.

A MODERN MIRACLE – AROUND THE WORLD IN 80 DAYS!

London to Suez, via Mont Cenis tunnel and Brindisi, Rail and Steamer	7 days
Suez to Bombay, by Steamer	13 days
Bombay to Calcutta, by Rail	3 days
Calcutta to Hong Kong, by Steamer	13 days
Hong Kong to Yokohama, by Steamer	6 days
Yokohama to San Francisco, by Steamer	22 days
San Francisco to New York, by Rail	7 days
New York to London, Steamer and Rail	9 days
TOTAL JOURNEY TIME	80 days

Thomas Flanagan, the brewery owner, chuckled. 'That's all very well, but in real life things would hardly go that smoothly! Why, an accident or some bad weather could easily add a week or more to the journey.'

'I'm afraid that Flanagan is right,' Andrew Stuart said. 'You are a clever man, Mr Fogg, but in this instance you are wrong. I'd bet £4,000 that it couldn't be done.'

Phileas Fogg saw the others nodding their heads.

'Very well,' he said with a smile. 'I have £20,000 deposited at Barings Bank. If the five of you are willing to wager £4,000 each, let us shake hands on the bet. The mail train to Dover leaves London at a quarter to nine tonight. Today is Wednesday 2nd October. If I am back in London in this very room in the Reform Club on Saturday 21st December by eight forty-five in the evening, I win. If not, my £20,000 is yours. I will write you a cheque for that amount – if I do not appear, you may cash it. Now, if you will excuse me, I will return to my house. My servant Passepartout will need time to prepare.'

Later that evening, as the Dover train left Charing Cross Station at eight forty-five precisely, Jean Passepartout sat opposite his master in a state of shock. He had only started

work as Phileas Fogg's servant that very morning, and he had applied for the position precisely because he was looking for peace and quiet.

Although he was only thirty years old, Passepartout had lived an exciting and adventurous life – including jobs as a circus trapeze artist and a fireman in Paris – and now he wanted to settle down. When he'd seen the vacancy advertised and made some enquiries about Mr Fogg, all that he could discover was that his new master was wealthy, and rarely if ever left London.

No one knew where Phileas Fogg's money had come from, or anything about his family, but he was understood to be a most respectable gentleman. Now it seemed that they were to go around the world – and at breakneck speed.

Passepartout hadn't even been allowed to pack a suitcase, just an overnight bag with a few clothes. 'We can buy what we need on our journey', Mr Fogg had said. He had also given Passepartout a small leather holdall to look after. It contained a copy of *Bradshaw's Continental Railway Steam Transit and General Guide* and £20,000 in banknotes. The £20,000 he had pledged as a bet, plus his £20,000 spending money, was all that Mr Fogg had in the world.

Seven days later, on 9th October, Phileas Fogg and Passepartout arrived at the town of Suez on the steamship *Mongolia*. Their journey across the English Channel, through Europe by train and then across the Mediterranean from Italy and down the Suez Canal had gone exactly as planned.

What neither of them knew was that during those seven days the man who had stolen £55,000 from the bank back in England had been identified as – Mr Phileas Fogg! Fogg's photograph – kept in the Reform Club along with those of all the other members – was found to correspond exactly with the bank clerk's description of the robber.

The description had been transmitted by telegraph to policemen who had been sent to guard all foreign ports. The officer stationed at Suez was Detective Fix, and he waited impatiently for the *Mongolia* to reach harbour. Fix reasoned that if Mr Fogg really was attempting to travel round the world in order to confuse the police who were on his track, then there was a good chance he might be on that steamship.

When the detective boarded the *Mongolia* and discovered that Phileas Fogg and his servant were indeed included in the passenger list, a smile lit up his shrewd intelligent face. He bought a ticket for Bombay, and sent a telegram to England asking the Police Commissioner to send an arrest warrant to the British consul's office in that city, where he could collect it. Bombay was a British territory, and once Fogg had arrived there he could be charged with the robbery – which wasn't possible in Suez. Unfortunately the

warrant could only get to Bombay *after* they had arrived. Fix hoped that he would be able to persuade the chief of police there to delay Fogg's departure until the warrant arrived.

The voyage of the *Mongolia* from Suez to Bombay – with a stop at Aden, to take on coal – was supposed to take thirteen days. Luckily the weather in the Indian Ocean was good. There had been a strong north-west wind, and the sails had been hoisted to supplement the propeller. So instead of the *Mongolia* arriving at Bombay on 22nd October, it reached that port two days early, on 20th October, at half past four in the afternoon.

Detective Fix went straight to the Bombay chief of police, who refused to arrest Phileas Fogg without a warrant. There was only one thing to be done, Fix thought – he would have to follow his suspect, around the world if necessary, and arrest him the moment they reached Britain again. When Fogg and his servant boarded the train to Calcutta, Detective Fix got into a different carriage. He did not want them to notice that he was following them.

Mr Fogg and his servant found that they were sharing a railway carriage with Brigadier General Sir Francis Cromarty, a British army officer who they had already met on board the *Mongolia*.

Sir Francis was amused to see that Phileas Fogg paid absolutely no attention to the fascinating sights they passed. On the second day of their journey, the train travelled through immense tracts of land extending as far as the eye could see. First they steamed through jungles in which tigers fled, scared at the roar and rattle of the train; then amongst forests where elephants watched the speeding train with a thoughtful stare. As for Mr Fogg, he spent his time reading his *Bradshaw* and making notes about the distance he had travelled, and the number of days he had left to complete his journey.

Then on 22nd October, at eight o'clock in the morning, the train stopped at the little village of Kholby.

The guard passed along the line, calling out 'All change here!'

'What on earth do you mean?' Sir Francis asked.

'The line is not yet finished beyond this point.'

Sir Francis was furious. 'Not finished! How can that be? We've bought tickets straight through from Bombay to Calcutta.'

'Yes sir, but it is understood that passengers make their own arrangements to travel between Kholby and Allahabad – no more than fifty miles. The line runs from there to Calcutta.'

Passepartout looked as if he would have liked to knock the guard down. Phileas Fogg, however, remained as calm as ever. He spoke to his servant.

'This will not affect our timetable. Remember that we got to Bombay two days early. We still have three more days to get to Calcutta.'

Mr Fogg, Sir Francis Cromarty and Passepartout then searched the town for some means of transport. Because most of the other passengers had known about the gap in the line all the carriages, ponies and so on had already been hired. Then Passepartout, who had been exploring on his own, returned with a solution. He had found an elephant! Its owner had no intention of taking them fifty miles across country to Allahabad, but as usual Phileas Fogg had the answer. He bought Kiouni – for that was the elephant's name – for the enormous sum of £2,000, and was lucky enough to find a young, intelligent *mahout* or elephant driver who would also act as their guide. One more person would make little difference to an elephant, so Mr Fogg invited Sir Francis to travel with him and his servant.

Meanwhile Detective Fix, who had managed to find a seat in a buffalo cart, had set off for Calcutta before them.

The young Indian was clearly a very skilful driver. He covered Kiouni's back with a kind of cloth saddle, and hung two large baskets down the creature's sides. Passepartout sat behind the *mahout* on the elephant's back, and Fogg and Sir Francis each occupied a basket.

The countryside they passed through soon became very wild. They rode through dense forests, then thickets of palm trees, and then large dry plains dotted with bushes and sprinkled with huge blocks of hard, crystalline stone.

That night the little group found some shelter in a ruined bungalow. The Indian driver made a fire with dead branches, and supper was prepared with some food that they had bought in Kholby. Kiouni slept on his feet, leaning against a large tree trunk.

By four o'clock in the afternoon of the second day – the 23rd October – the three travellers and their guide were only eight miles from the station at Allahabad. They were passing through a dense forest, when suddenly Kiouni appeared nervous, and stopped in his tracks. Fortunately the elephant had halted behind a dense clump of trees, which allowed Mr Fogg and his companions to observe the scene that followed without being seen.

A procession passed them about fifty yards away, to the sound of chanting, beating drums and clashing cymbals. At the head of the column was a group of priests, wearing tall hats and long robes, surrounded by a crowd of men, women and children. These were followed by a painted statue of a figure with four arms, carried in a richly decorated ox cart.

'That is the goddess Kali,' Sir Francis Cromarty whispered.

A number of holy men followed the ox cart, dancing and twirling about, together with another group of priests in colourful robes. The priests were dragging a woman along with them, who looked dazed and stumbled with each step.

The woman was young and beautiful. Her tunic was decorated with gold lace, and she was covered with jewels, bracelets and rings.

A squad of armed guards armed with swords and pistols marched behind the young woman, carrying a dead body. The corpse was that of an old man, dressed in the rich clothes of a rajah – an Indian prince. The final members of the procession were a band of musicians.

Sir Francis Cromarty turned to the Indian guide with a sad expression.

'Is it a suttee?'

The young man nodded and put his finger to his lips.

After the procession had disappeared into the forest, Phileas Fogg asked the young *mahout* to explain. He told the Englishman that a 'suttee' was an ancient Indian ceremony in which a widow would join her husband on the funeral pyre when his body was burnt. Such ceremonies were now very rare. Usually the women involved in a suttee would agree to take part, but sometimes they were forced to sacrifice themselves. In this case, the whole countryside knew that the woman they had seen – Princess Aouda – was an unwilling victim, and had been drugged to make her quiet.

'She is being taken to the temple at Pillaji, two miles from here,' the Indian said. 'She is to spend the night there, under guard, and will be sacrificed tomorrow morning at first light.'

'Then we must rescue her,' said Mr Fogg.

'Well! So you do have some feelings, after all!' exclaimed Sir Francis.

'Sometimes,' replied Phileas Fogg. 'When I have time to spare.'

As it turned out, saving the princess from her horrible fate was much more difficult than any of the travellers might have imagined. She was so closely guarded that it was impossible to enter the temple to rescue her. As day dawned, Sir Francis Cromarty – who was hiding near the temple with Phileas Fogg and the *mahout* – broke the silence.

'Where is your servant, Fogg?' he asked. 'When the princess is brought out to the funeral pyre, we'll all need to do something. But what?'

At that moment the temple doors opened, and Princess Aouda was brought out. She was dragged to her husband's funeral pyre, where the rajah lay upon a pile of sandalwood, saturated with perfumed oil. The princess was forced to lie down beside him.

A blazing torch was applied to the wood, which burst into flame. Then suddenly a cry of terror arose from those gathered around the fire. The old rajah was not dead after all! There he was standing upright upon the fiery funeral pile, clasping his young wife in his arms, ready to leap from amid the smoke into the midst of the horror-stricken crowd.

The priests, guards and other onlookers were seized with fear, and threw themselves face down onto the ground, thinking that the rajah's spirit had come to life.

The rajah ran swiftly towards Mr Fogg and his two companions, who looked on in astonishment. When he reached them they saw that he was – Passepartout!

Phileas Fogg realised that the clever Frenchman must have hidden himself in the funeral pyre during the night.

Before the frightened mourners had realised that they had been tricked, the travellers – taking Princess Aouda with them – had returned to the clump of trees where they had left Kiouni. The sound of shouts and gunfire faded behind them as they set off on the last leg of their journey to the railway station in Allahabad.

The elephant now had one more passenger to carry, but it made little difference to the immensely strong animal. Mr Fogg had decided that when they arrived at Allahabad, he would give the valuable creature to the *mahout* as a present. That way the young Indian would be properly rewarded for his service, and Kiouni would be well looked after.

Now that Princess Aouda had escaped from the suttee, she would never be safe in India. She was grateful that Phileas Fogg had offered to take her with him to Europe, where she could stay with her uncle in Holland.

The train from Allahabad reached Calcutta on 25th October. Sir Francis Cromarty had already left the train at Benares, to rejoin his regiment.

As the carriage drew into the station, Phileas Fogg opened his notebook and showed it to Passepartout and the princess.

'This is the schedule I drew up when we left London,' he said. 'As you can see, we are exactly on time. The *Rangoon* leaves for Hong Kong this afternoon. The two days we lost between Bombay and Calcutta were made up for by the two we gained from Suez to Bombay.'

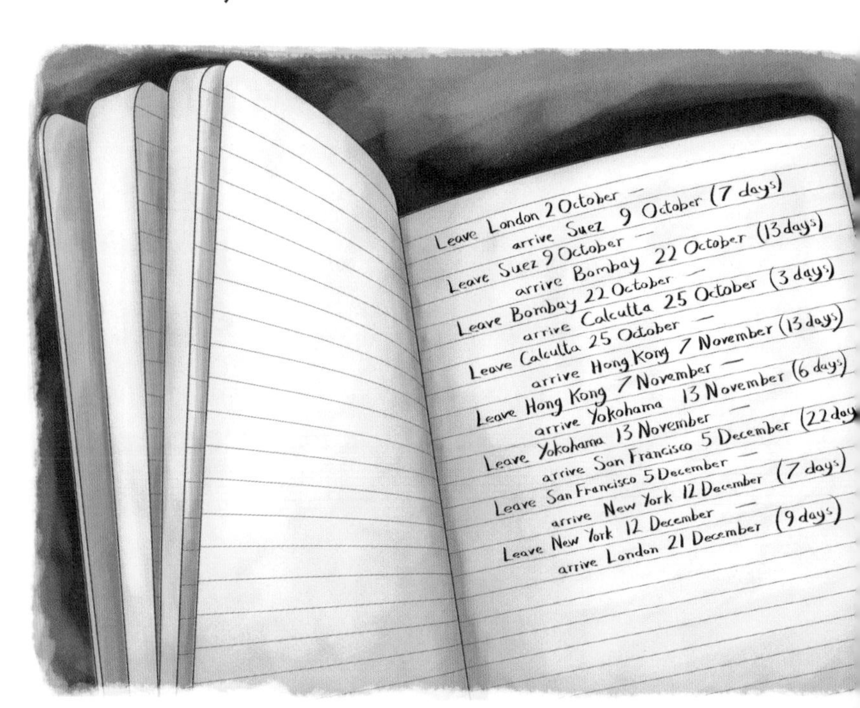

Fogg's words made Passepartout much happier. However, the travellers were unaware that Detective Fix had arrived in Calcutta the day before, and was waiting for Phileas Fogg to get there. Fix had not yet received a warrant for Fogg's arrest so when the three boarded the *Rangoon* for their journey to Hong Kong, the detective followed them, taking care to keep out of their sight. He hoped that by the time they all reached Hong Kong the arrest warrant would have arrived.

So far in his journey around the world Phileas Fogg had benefited from good weather. He knew that this could not go on forever, and sure enough the high winds and rough seas that they now experienced meant that the journey from Calcutta to Hong Kong on the *Rangoon* took fourteen days instead of thirteen.

They arrived on 8th November, a day late, and found that the *Carnatic* – the Yokohama steamship – had left Hong Kong the day before.

Passepartout was desolate at the delay. There would of course be another ship that they could catch in a few days' time, but that would be of no use to them – his master had to reach the Japanese port of Yokohama by 13th November, otherwise they would miss the steamer to San Francisco which left on that date.

As usual, Phileas Fogg seemed quite unworried by the setback, and set off towards the docks to try to find another boat that was ready to leave. A powerful vessel might still get them to Yokohama in time.

After a short search Phileas Fogg discovered the *Tankadère*, a small but fast pilot boat. She was about twenty tons and built like a racing yacht. The crew consisted of the captain, John Bunsby, and four seamen.

When Mr Fogg asked if they could take him to Yokohama by 13th November, the captain shook his head.

'No sir, that's quite impossible. Even the *Tankadère* is not that fast. But there is another solution to your problem. The *General Grant* – that's the San Francisco steamer – leaves from Shanghai on 11th November before it goes on to Yokohama. With luck we can get to Shanghai in time for you to join the steamer there.'

Phileas Fogg nodded. 'Very well. I can offer you £100 a day and an extra £200 if we catch the steamer.'

The two men shook hands on the deal. Then as Phileas Fogg, Passepartout and Princess Aouda were about to go aboard, an anxious-looking figure approached them.

'Excuse me sir, were you one of the passengers on the *Rangoon*, like me? Forgive my asking, but if you've managed to find a boat to Yokohama, I'd be willing to pay if I can share it with you.'

Mr Fogg saw no reason to refuse the stranger.

'Of course, my dear sir, you are very welcome to join us. We aim to meet the steamer at Shanghai.'

The additional passenger thanked him and boarded the *Tankadère*. He was, of course, Detective Fix.

A voyage in a small vessel from Hong Kong to Shanghai through the China Seas at that time of year could be dangerous, but Phileas Fogg trusted the captain's experience. The sails were

stretched out overhead like great wings, and the *Tankadère* ran before the wind like a speeding bird.

The following day a hurricane burst upon them. Fortunately the storm was behind them, and although the schooner was almost lifted out of the water by the tempest, she shot towards her destination at full speed. The passengers were drenched with spray, and at times they were almost swallowed up in the monstrous waves.

Princess Aouda put up with the conditions bravely. She glanced admiringly at Phileas Fogg, who seemed as cool and calm as ever. He may not say much, she thought, but he is always confident and determined. She was becoming very interested in that gentleman's plans.

Finally the storm blew itself out, and the *Tankadère* arrived at Shanghai in time for the travellers to transfer to the *General Grant*. The steamer would call in briefly at the Japanese port of Yokohama before starting the long voyage across the Pacific Ocean to San Francisco, on the west coast of the United States of America.

All went according to plan for Phileas Fogg – but not for Detective Fix. When they arrived at Yokohama the detective went ashore to the English consul's office. The arrest warrant for Phileas Fogg had arrived, but it was useless, as they were no longer in British territory. There was only one thing for Fix to do: he must get back on board the *General Grant*, follow his suspect all the way to England, and arrest him there.

The *General Grant* was a powerful paddle-steamer which also had three masts and a large spread of sail. Even if the weather had been bad she would be expected to arrive at San Francisco in twenty-two days.

During the voyage Princess Aouda became more and more attracted to Phileas Fogg. She was of course grateful for his kindness in allowing her to travel with them, but her feelings were deeper than that. As for Mr Fogg, he seemed not to notice her interest.

At seven o'clock in the morning on 5th December, exactly according to their original schedule, Phileas Fogg, Passepartout and Princess Aouda set foot on American soil. Detective Fix had met up with them again during the voyage, and invented a suitable story to explain his journey. Phileas Fogg, suspecting nothing, agreed that he could travel back to England with them.

Their train was due to leave San Francisco at six o'clock that evening, so the travellers had time to see something of that large city. Passepartout looked with great interest at the wide streets, the rows of lofty houses, the churches and other places of worship, immense docks, and countless cabs, omnibuses, and tramway-cars. Americans, Europeans, Chinese, and Indians filled the streets, making up a population of over two hundred thousand.

'Should I buy some guns?' Passepartout asked his master. 'I hear that the Indian tribes hold up trains like highwaymen!'

'I cannot imagine we will have any trouble,' Phileas Fogg replied. 'But do so by all means, if it makes you feel happier.'

It would take seven days to cross America from west to east. The track had only been completed three years ago – before that, the same journey took six months or more.

That night their carriage turned into a comfortable sleeping car. The backs of the seats folded down to make beds, with thick curtains dividing off each space.

The next morning the train entered the Sierra Nevada mountain range. There were few tunnels or bridges on this part of the route, and the track followed all the curves of the mountains, sometimes running along the edge of a cliff and at others plunging into narrow valleys.

When the Sierras had been left behind, the route led across the great plains of America. Here tens of thousands of bison roamed – if they crossed the track, a train could be held up for hours. But then on the third day a much more dangerous threat appeared – one that made Passepartout glad that he had bought six revolvers in San Francisco.

The first sign of the sudden attack by a band of Sioux warriors was the sound of firing from outside the whole length of the train, accompanied by wild shouts and screams. The Sioux, riding alongside the train, were equipped with rifles – most of the passengers were carrying pistols, and fired back.

From the moment the attack began, Princess Aouda showed great bravery. Armed with one of Passepartout's revolvers, and standing next to Phileas Fogg, she fired through a broken window whenever an attacker appeared.

Detective Fix also fought courageously. But then disaster struck. Two of the Sioux warriors had got inside the cab of the engine, and had clubbed down the driver and fireman. The next station was only two miles away, and contained a garrison of American soldiers. If the train didn't stop there, it would be many more miles to the next station – by which time the Sioux would have killed every passenger on board.

Fortunately Passepartout was quick-thinking as well as brave. He made his way to the front of the train, but instead of trying to recapture the engine, he managed to uncouple it from the first carriage. The engine sped onwards, and the carriages – without any power to pull them – slowed and stopped just beyond the soldiers' fort.

The Sioux warriors did not remain to fight the American soldiers and rode off. Passepartout had saved everyone on board.

Once Phileas Fogg, the princess and Fix had finished thanking Passepartout, the travellers realised that although they were safe, their plan to reach New York by 12th December was now at risk. It might take a day or more for the staff at the next station to discover that something was wrong, and send a new engine back along the track.

As it happened the engine returned at midnight. The driver and fireman had not been killed, and had managed to stop the engine fifty miles further down the line, where they had been treated for their injuries. The carriages were linked up again immediately, and the train set off at full speed.

Phileas Fogg and his companions finally reached New York on 12th December – but not until just before midnight. At last the Hudson River came into view, and the train pulled up in front of the pier. As soon as they left the train they spoke to the harbourmaster. The *China*, bound for Liverpool, had left forty-five minutes earlier! No other fast steamer was due to leave New York for several days.

Phileas Fogg did not show any anxiety. 'Then we must find another boat,' he said. 'Wait here while I search the docks.'

When Mr Fogg returned, he announced that he had discovered a propeller-driven cargo vessel, the *Henrietta*, a powerful craft that was owned by Captain Speedy. The captain had absolutely refused to take the Englishman and his companions to England – until Fogg offered him the huge sum of $8,000. Within an hour they had left New York for Liverpool.

The *Henrietta* was as fast as she looked, and thanks to fine weather they seemed sure to get to Liverpool by 21st December. The powerful engines, assisted when the wind allowed by a set of try-sails, set an excellent pace. Then, after eight days and with three hundred miles further to go, the ship's engineer spoke to Phileas Fogg.

'I'm sorry, sir, but we don't have enough coal left to get to Liverpool, not at this speed. We've been steaming full speed for days. Shall I order the engine room to slow down?'

Phileas shook his head. 'By no means. Ask the captain to step up on deck. I have a proposition to make to him.'

A few minutes later the captain stood in front of him. 'Captain Speedy, please listen very carefully to what I have to say. I want to buy your ship. Name your price.'

The captain laughed. 'And where will you get the money from, in mid-Atlantic? This ship is worth $50,000 dollars.'

'Very well, Captain. Here is $60,000!'

Phileas opened the leather case that he always carried with him, and reached inside for a bundle of notes. Passepartout, watching from close by, was horrified. Surely at this rate his master would have spent all his money long before reaching their goal.

The captain's eyes opened wide. 'All right, sir. The ship is yours. But what do you intend to do with her?'

Phileas Fogg chuckled. 'I intend to burn her. All the wooden deck and fittings, that is. When we reach land, I expect that only the engines and the iron hull will be left. You are welcome to keep those, as well as your $60,000.'

Phileas wasn't joking. As soon as the last lump of coal had run out, the crew were told to start chopping up the furniture and wooden fittings. When they had gone, the thick wooden deck was ripped up to feed the hungry engines.

All that time the *Henrietta* was sailing

at full steam. Just when the last pieces of wood were being fed into the boilers, the captain spotted the west coast of Ireland. Knowing the ship could steam no further, Phileas Fogg ordered the captain to enter the nearest harbour. They had reached the port of Queenstown.

The passengers quickly disembarked, Phileas first, followed by Passepartout, Princess Aouda, and Detective Fix.

'We can take the express mail train to Dublin, and then a fast boat to Liverpool,' Phileas said.

And that was what they did. At twenty minutes to midday on 21st December, Phileas Fogg and the others set foot on Liverpool docks. They were only six hours away from London.

Detective Fix seized the moment. He put his hand on Phileas Fogg's shoulder.

'Are you Phileas Fogg?' he asked.

'Yes, sir, I am.'

'Then in the name of Her Majesty the Queen, you are under arrest and must follow me to the nearest police station.'

For two and a half hours Phileas Fogg sat on a hard bench in one of the cells in Liverpool Central police station, calmly reading a novel. Passepartout and Princess Aouda, who were in a waiting room nearby, had insisted that there must be some mistake, but Detective Fix was triumphant.

Then came a telegram for Fix from the Metropolitan Police. Its effect on the detective was immediate. At twenty-seven minutes to three Detective Fix burst into the cell where Phileas Fogg was being held.

'My dear sir! I am very sorry ... the bank robber was arrested three days ago ... an unfortunate resemblance ... you are free to go!'

Phileas Fogg, Passepartout and the princess raced to the station as fast as a cab could take them – to find that they had just missed the 2.45 express to London.

Mr Fogg then hired a special train at great expense. It left at three o'clock, and after promising the engine driver a bonus, Phileas Fogg sped off towards London with his faithful servant and Princess Aouda.

They had five and a half hours to get to London. This was perfectly possible if the line was clear all the way. Unfortunately there were some unavoidable delays, and by the time the travellers reached Euston Station, all the clocks were showing ten minutes to nine. Phileas Fogg had lost his bet!

That evening Phileas Fogg returned to his house in Savile Row. He asked Passepartout to set aside a room in the house for Princess Aouda, and to see that she had all she needed.

For the whole of the next day – Sunday – Mr Fogg remained shut in his room. The princess became more and more worried. He had lost all his money. Might he try to kill himself, in desperation?

At last, at about half past seven in the evening, Mr Fogg asked to see her.

'I have brought you all the way from India to this country, and now I have lost everything,' he said sadly. 'I have nothing that I can offer you.'

The princess smiled. 'But you have!' she said kindly. 'Mr Fogg, two people can bear poverty better than one. Would you like me to be your wife?'

For once in his life Phileas Fogg was completely surprised.

'Of course!' he said. 'For I love you truly.'

Passepartout was sent for, and told to visit the Reverend Samuel Wilson, vicar of the local parish.

'It's only five past eight,' said Fogg. 'Please tell the vicar that we need a licence to get married tomorrow, as early as is possible on a Monday morning.'

It was after half past eight that evening before Passepartout returned to Savile Row, amazed and out of breath.

'Sir— Madam— !' he shouted. 'I had to wait for the vicar ... and when he arrived ... he told me that tomorrow is not Monday ... it is *Sunday*! So today is Saturday ... '

Phileas Fogg laughed. 'But of course it is! And there is still time for me to save my £20,000. We must take a cab to the Reform Club immediately.'

On the way Mr Fogg explained to Passepartout what had happened. 'I was a fool to forget,' he said. 'It's well known that if anyone travels right round the globe from west to east, they lose a day in the process. Travelling towards the sun means that sunset arrives a little earlier each day. Of course each country we passed through adjusts its time accordingly, but in such small increments that we did not notice that each day was very slightly shorter.'

Phileas Fogg arrived at his club with seconds to spare, and so won his bet. He was £20,000 richer – but had spent almost as much on the journey.

'So you have gained nothing?' a friend at the club asked.

'Hardly nothing. I have gained a charming wife. Isn't that enough reward for travelling around the world?'

LOOKING CLOSER

Great readers!

This retelling of Verne's much loved story gives readers of any age and reading ability a taste of a great classic which may inspire you to get to know this and other works better. Read the full novel in all its original power and splendour in one of the many complete translations available, from bargain paperbacks to beautifully bound hardbacks. You may well find a copy in your local library. If you can read French, or if you ever decide to study the language, the original title is *Le Tour du Monde en Quatre-Vingts Jours.*

Filling in the spaces

The loss of so many of Jules Verne's original words is a sad but necessary part of the shortening process. We have had to make some difficult decisions, omitting subplots and details, some important, some less so, but all interesting. We have also, at times, taken the liberty of combining two events into one, or of giving a character words or actions that originally belong to another. The points below will fill in some of the gaps, but nothing can beat the original.

- When Detective Fix is following Phileas Fogg he makes friends with Passepartout, who is not sure whether or not his master really is the bank robber.

- In Bombay Passepartout visits a mosque, and does not realise that he has to take off his shoes when he enters the holy place. He manages to escape from two angry priests who chase him. Fix takes the priests with him to Bombay and Passepartout is arrested, but Phileas Fogg pays £2,000 bail and Passepartout does not go to prison.

- After the travellers arrive at Hong Kong, Fix gets Passepartout drunk and drugged with opium. Passepartout travels to Hong Kong on a different boat. When he gets there he has no money and joins a troupe of acrobats until Phileas Fogg finds him.

- The *Tankadère* gets delayed when the wind drops and, before it reaches Shanghai, Phileas Fogg and his companions see the *General Grant* leaving harbour on the way to Yokohama. The crew of the *Tankadère* signal to the steamer, which stops and picks up the travellers.

- In New York Phileas Fogg and his companions attend a political rally which turns into a riot. Fogg has a disagreement with an American, Colonel Proctor. The two men are about to fight a duel on the train but are interrupted by the attack of the Sioux warriors.

- After Passepartout uncouples the carriages he is captured by the Sioux, and Phileas Fogg has to rescue him. This makes Fogg and his companions miss the train, and they hire a large sail-powered sledge to travel over the snow and ice to Chicago. They then catch a train from Chicago to New York.

- Captain Speedy refuses to take the travellers to Liverpool – he will only take them to Bordeaux, on the French coast. After the *Henrietta* leaves New York, Phileas Fogg shuts the captain below deck until he offers to buy the boat from him, and they land at Queenstown (now known as Cobh) on the west coast of Ireland.

- In the original story we are given a more detailed scientific explanation about why the travellers' journey round the world from west to east will mean that they 'lose' a day.

- Jules Verne's original version of *Around the World in Eighty Days* contains some contradictions about dates and times. In this version some of the dates have been altered slightly to make sure that the timetable that Phileas Fogg follows fits the journey times.

Back in time

It is now possible to travel around the world using normal passenger airline routes in less than three days, including stops on the ground. This might make Phileas Fogg's journey seem rather ordinary, but when *Around the World in Eighty Days* was first published in France as a newspaper serial in 1872 its readers were fascinated by Fogg's achievement.

Phileas Fogg's fictional journey was based on real timetables, although a few years earlier it would have been impossible. Before the Suez Canal was opened in 1869, ships from England to India would have had to sail right round the southern tip of Africa, adding five thousand miles to the journey. The railroad linking the west and east coasts of America was also completed in 1869, saving six months of travel, and the Mont Cenis Tunnel under the Alps opened in 1871. It was not until the 1860s that suitable steam engines were developed for ocean crossings. In the days of sail, and before the Suez Canal was opened, a voyage from England to India took at least six months – by 1872 this journey could be done in three weeks.

When *Around the World in Eighty Days* was published in book form in 1873 it quickly became a best-seller, and was translated into many languages. As well as the novelty of fast and relatively safe travel, readers were gripped by Jules Verne's descriptions of the exotic countries visited by Phileas Fogg and his companions. In the twenty-first century we are used to foreign travel, but when Verne wrote his book most people never left their own country unless they worked abroad. His vivid descriptions of Arabian ports, the Far East and the American West introduced his readers to scenes that few could ever hope to experience in real life.

Finding out more

We recommend the following books and websites to gain a greater understanding of Jules Verne and the world he lived in.

Books

- Arthur C. Clarke and Gonzague Saint Bris, *The World of Jules Verne*, Turtle Point Press, 2007.
- Jules Verne, *Journey to the Centre of the Earth*,
- Jules Verne, *Twenty Thousand Leagues under the Sea*

Websites

- www.julesverne.ca

This site is aimed at book collectors, but it contains lots of information about the author, including photographs.

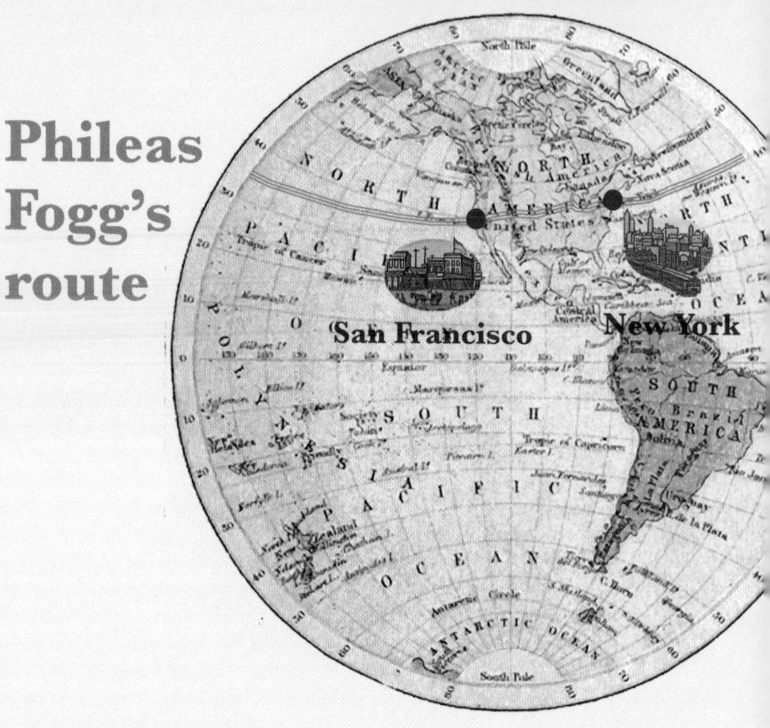

- www.najvs.org

Includes a list of most of Jules Verne's books.

Films

- *Around the World in Eighty Days* (1956), United Artists, directed by Michael Anderson.

If you are able to see this film you will see that the story has been altered in a number of ways. Why do you think these changes have been made?

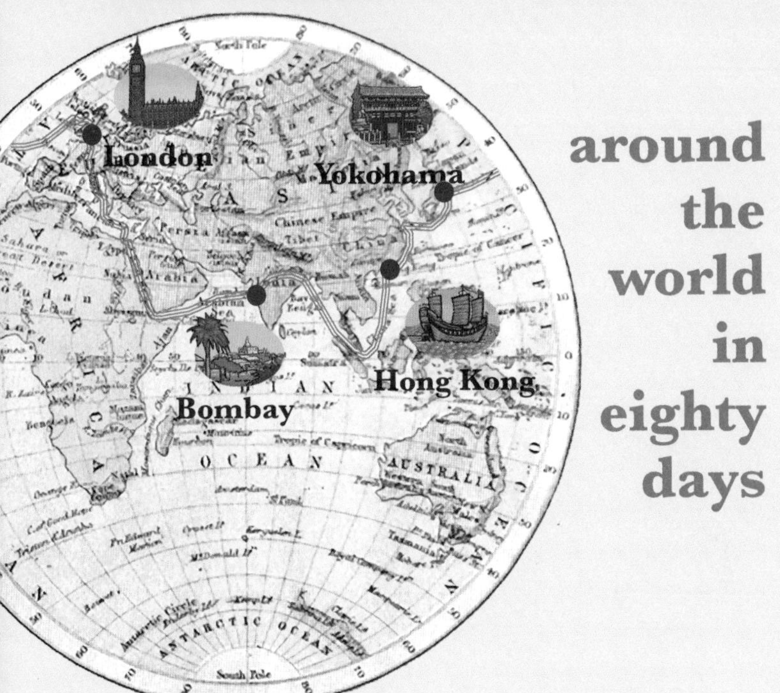

Food for thought

Here are a few things to think about if you are reading *Around the World in Eighty Days* alone or ideas for discussion if you are reading it with friends.

In this retelling of *Around the World in Eighty Days* we have tried to recreate, as accurately as possible, Jules Verne's original plot and characters. We have also tried to imitate aspects of his style. Remember, however, that this is not the original work; thinking about the points below, therefore, can help you to begin to understand

Jules Verne's craft. To move forward from here, turn to the full-length version of *Around the World in Eighty Days* and lose yourself in his exciting and imaginative story.

Starting points

- At the start of the book, Phileas Fogg is presented as a very calm, calculating person who never gets excited. How does his character develop during the story?

- The story is made more interesting by the imaginative ways that Phileas Fogg and Passepartout solve the problems that they face. Can you think of any examples?

- In some of the films of this book, the travellers use a balloon for part of the journey. Why do you think Jules Verne did *not* feature a balloon in his original version?

- The practice of suttee described in the book was very rare by 1872, and was also against the law. Why do you think Jules Verne included the suttee episode?

- Today the long-distance traveller usually goes by air. Is this a good or bad thing? What might we have lost compared with the nineteenth-century experience of travel?

Themes

What you think Jules Verne is saying about the following themes in *Around the World in Eighty Days*?

- the power of money
- the achievements of technology
- the relationship between master and servant
- persistence and self-belief

Style

Can you find paragraphs containing examples of the following?

- a description of someone's actions which tells us something about their character
- the use of charts or lists to make the story easier to follow
- descriptions of exotic or unusual places or events which allow the reader to visualise them in detail
- dialogue which shows a person's state of mind, such as excitement or fear

Look closely at how these paragraphs are written. What do you notice? Can you write a paragraph in the same style?

Great Reads for all Ages!

The world's greatest classic stories come to life in these expert retellings.

Baker Street Readers give an enchanting taste of the original tales, quoting best-known lines and most memorable moments, all supported with wonderfully witty (and sometimes scary!) illustrations.

other classics to explore...

Dickens & Austen

Wells, Shelley & Shakespeare